Real Mummies Don't Bleed
Friendly Tales for October Nights

Susan Whitcher

Real Mummies
Don't Bleed

FRIENDLY TALES
for OCTOBER NIGHTS

Pictures by Andrew Glass

Farrar · Straus · Giroux   New York

This book is not complete without an acknowledgment of
Mr. Alan Davidson's excellent book *Mediterranean Seafood*
(Penguin Books, 1972), which provided the menu for
Solly's Eastern Carryout Restaurant. I have made and
enjoyed Ochtapódi Krassáto *often*. Mr. Davidson is also
my source for the name Mahmuzlu Camgöz, which is not
actually a person's name but the Turkish word for a
variety of small shark, or dogfish.
—S.W.

Library of Congress catalog card number: 93-7953
Published simultaneously in Canada by HarperCollins*CanadaLtd*
Printed in the United States of America
Designed by Martha Rago
First edition, 1993

For my old Baltimore writers' group,
their heirs, assigns, and residual legatees
—S.W.

For Alice Finney Gabbard
A dollar every January
for as long as I can remember
—A.G.

Contents

Hieroglyphics
3

Annie's Pet Witch
29

Mystery of the One-eyed Dog
49

The Paper Bag Genie
75

Toad Meets Frankenstein
107

Real Mummies Don't Bleed
Friendly Tales for October Nights

Hieroglyphics

A REAL MUMMY WOULDN'T bleed, any more than a salami. Because, see, they took out all the blood and the guts and put it in these little jars. Then they packed the mummy body full of salt and pepper and stuff so it dried up, just like a salami. I explained all this to Lauren Schwartz. She lives next door to me, and I have known her practically ever since we were babies, in kindergarten. But the thing is, she never listens to me.

Lauren made a mummy costume for the Handi-Mart costume parade the weekend before Halloween. She painted stupid blood all down the front. Then she went and won second prize for kids under thirteen. Those judges must just love ketchup.

Anyway, I think it's stupid the way people make a big fuss about mummies, just because there's supposed to be a dead body inside. It's not like you see anything except a bunch of old torn-up sheets. Because the really fancy part, the part that somebody might actually want to look at, is the box they put them in. The Egyptians made their coffins to look like statues of the dead person, with gold and decorations and hieroglyphics all over. Hieroglyphics are picture writing. I told everybody that's what I was going to be for Halloween, the mummy's coffin.

It's called a sarcophagus. I went to the library, but all their Egypt books were totally baby, with huge print, or else like college books, with maps and graphs in them instead of real pictures. I was getting practically desperate when I found this real old book. It was lying on the bottom shelf by itself because it was too big to stand up with the others, and it wasn't even in English, but it sure had neat pictures. Especially of the sarcophaguses. Lots of them showed the picture writing, which is what I needed to copy off of. I was surprised the librarian let me take it out, actually. It was so old and heavy.

So this is how I made the costume. The headdress part was easy, I just took a striped guest towel and wrapped a rubber snake around it kind of like a sweatband. The important thing with an Egyptian headdress is not to cover your ears. If your ears don't stick out, it doesn't look like in the pictures. The snake cost $3.49 (plus tax) of my own money at Handi-Mart.

For the sarcophagus body I used an old garment bag. Actually, this was my mother's idea, but it turned out really neat anyway. My mother was an airline flight attendant before she had the twins, so she had this kind of stiff cloth bag that she used to cover her uniforms on a hanger. I turned the zipper around to the back so I could paint on the front. My mother let me paint it gold and cut slits for my arms.

The gold paint took a whole two days to dry, and even then it smelled like a gas station and stuck to the newspapers a little. So it wasn't until after school on Halloween that I got around to the picture writing.

I used red and black permanent markers. See, the hieroglyphics were supposed to be like prayers and secret passwords and stuff to help the dead person get into the Afterlife. Don't ask me what my hieroglyphics really said, of course. I just copied the ones I liked from the old library book.

I took a long time, too, because I really wanted to do a good job. By the time I finished, it was practically dark and the first trick-or-treaters were already going around in our neighborhood. I could hear them laughing and calling to each other outside. My mother had the light on in the kitchen. She was letting Danny and Tammy— they're the twins—scoop the glop out of their pumpkin.

I stood up, feeling kind of stiff and rubbing my eyes from working in the dark room. My hieroglyphics came out better than I expected. It was almost like all those pictures of snakes and eyes and birds and sideways people were alive and glowing and changing their places on the gold background.

When the doorbell chimed, I jumped like I'd gone to sleep or something, which maybe I did, because the hieroglyphics looked all right again now, flat and quiet. I pulled the costume on over my head and felt around for my arm and head holes. I could hear the tac-tac of my mother's heels across the hall, on her way to answer the door.

My mother flipped the light on in my room. "Rachel, your friends are waiting for you out on the sidewalk."

"What friends?" I said, blinking at the light.

See, I always used to go out with Lauren, because, after all, she does live right next door. But after she said what she did about my shorts in gym, I said I would go with Hilary Vogelman instead. Not that I cared all that much what Lauren said, even if it wasn't very nice, because it is a fact of life that lots of people my age put on weight, and it is only because they are developing and does not mean they are going to be fat when they grow up. Even my mother says this, and she used to be an airline flight attendant. What bothered me was, Hilary Vogelman had been home sick for three days with strep throat. So I wondered who else was out there.

I thought about this while I arranged the towel over my hair and wrapped the snake around it. The snake kept trying to sproing off, because it was rubber.

"You look terrific!" said my mother. She al-

ways says that so I will get Self Esteem. But
then she started saying, "I was never so amazed
in my life when I opened the door and saw all
those Egyptians! You kids are so creative. I wish
to goodness I'd bought more film for my camera . . ."

"Mom," I said, "who are you talking about?"

"Your friends, of course. Now close your eyes
and I'll put on a little black liner."

I closed my eyes. I could hear the twins starting a fight in the kitchen. Danny wanted a funny
face on the pumpkin, Tammy a scary one.

"Danny, wait for me, honey," called my
mother.

I tried again. "Mom, who?—"

"No, no, Tammy— Wait for Mother!"

Then the snake unwrapped suddenly, and the
tip of the tail flicked my eye, making it water.

"Don't rub it! Don't rub it!" screeched my
mother, grabbing my chin with one hand while
she gouged at my eye with a Kleenex. "Stay still,
Rachel, for goodness' sakes. And remember,
nine-thirty is the absolute latest. After that I call
the police, and the ambulance—tuck another tis-
sue in your sleeve, and don't forget— Tammy!
Put that knife down!"

I decided it was a waste of time trying to ask her questions. She must've got it wrong about my Egyptian friends, anyway. I took a bag for trick or treat and went out on the sidewalk to find out for myself who was there.

They were waiting for me a few doors down. My mother only got it half wrong. They were Egyptians all right, but the closer I got, the less they looked like any Egyptians I ever met before. The streetlight picked out glints like real gold on their clothes. Except some of them were not wearing much clothes but just jewelry on bare chests and arms. I got a cold feeling looking at them, like maybe the garment-bag zipper let the cold go down my back.

Or maybe it was their faces that made me feel that way. Because they were definitely not all regular people faces. One of them at least had a dog head. I don't mean like a mask, but a real dog, a kind of stripy-browny-yellow one with sharp ears that pricked forward. But the weirdest thing about those faces was, the harder I looked at them, the less sure I was of what I saw. It was like they were really a lot further away than I thought.

My mouth went dry, and my heart was starting

to bump. I turned and pounded up the steps to the nearest house and I pounded on the door. And I was rattling the door screen and kicking the bottom of it, and then somebody finally came, and I opened my mouth and I screamed:

"Trick or treat."

It was not what I meant to say at all.

"Oooh, don't you look gorgeous," said old Mrs. Porter. It was her house. "Who are you, King Tut?"

She had a bowl of Milky Way bars and she gave me one for myself and some extras, for my friends, she said. I said thank you. Then I stumped back down the steps to where the Egyptians were waiting on the sidewalk.

I have an idea about this. You know how in dreams weird stuff keeps happening but you just go with the flow like it was all totally normal? The thing is, maybe it's not just the dream makes you act that way. Maybe it's the weirdness. In real life not enough really weird things usually happen, so you might find it hard to check this idea out.

Anyway, I went down our street with the Egyptians. They were not a chatty bunch. I stopped at the Lees' and the Spinellis' and the

Vogelmans', and rung the bells and said trick or treat.

"Don't your friends want anything?" asked Mrs. Lee and Mr. Spinelli and Mrs. Vogelman. They poured treats into my bag, "to share."

"You kids are always so creative!" said Mrs. Vogelman, giving me a big smile. There is something definitely not right about Mrs. Vogelman's smile. It's like her teeth were all made in one piece and somebody just drew in the spaces between them with a pencil. Her hair is all one piece, too, like a Ken doll. I began to wonder if Mrs. Vogelman was an alien. Everything looked weird to me anymore.

Hilary was leaning over the banisters in her pink baby-doll pajamas. "What're you supposed to be?" she said.

"King Tut," I told her. There didn't seem much point in explaining to a bunch of aliens.

After the Vogelmans' it seemed a lot darker outside. I walked a long way with the Egyptians. My bag got heavy with stuff. We came to a neighborhood I didn't know. The houses were all a long ways apart and nobody had their porch lights on.

There weren't any streetlights, either. Actu-

ally, there wasn't any street. We were walking on sand. Cold sand plowed over the tops of my shoes. I ate a Milky Way bar from my treat bag. I ate three. All around us was sand, nothing but sand to the edge of the sky. The Egyptians began to sing.

I don't exactly remember coming to the river. Maybe I was asleep on my feet by that time. But actually what I think is, it was the singing that took us there, not the way people go on their feet or in cars, but more like the way music moves, without touching anything or taking up any space. Anyway, there was the river looking wide as the sand, only a shinier color dark.

A boat was pulled up on the bank. It looked like the moon. I mean, it curved up at both ends like the moon, but the main thing was, it sort of shone, too, without any kind of lights that I could see. Also, I didn't see any oars or sails or anything to make it move, but by this time I was so weirded out I didn't even think about it. I just got in when the others did. There was a kind of awning of striped cloth near the back and I got under that. The others took their places all along the boat, and it floated out on the water. I think they sang to it to make it go.

I can't say what it was about that singing; it was awfully beautiful, but it made me feel so sad. And lonely. I got to feeling so bad, it was like I died and was never going back to the shore, or to where there were lights and people's voices and Danny and Tammy having a spoon fight with the pumpkin glop. I hugged my knees up under my sarcophagus and wondered if it was possible to be dead without noticing.

"Don't cry," said a sniffly voice beside me in the dark place under the awning.

"Who's crying?" I said. "You're the one that's crying."

"I am not!"

"Are too," I said, feeling around in the dark near me. "Where are you, anyway?"

"Here."

Just then my hand touched something sticky. I jerked it away. Then a pale form loomed up from the shadows. It was a mummy. The mummy leaned towards me. I could see its eyes gleaming through a slit in the bandages. Something dark oozed down its bandaged front.

Something dark, and sticky, was smeared on my hand. I knew what it was now. Blood.

I said, "I swear to God, Lauren, you practically scared me to death!"

"I did?"

"Well, you don't need to sound so pleased about it," I told her. "What are you doing here, anyway?"

"I came with him," she said, pointing to a kind of throne near the front of the boat where a figure sat all wrapped up in white, almost like a mummy himself. I couldn't see his face from where we were, but I saw his crown, like a chef's tall hat, with red ears sticking out the sides. Or maybe they were feathers. It might've looked funny if he didn't sit so still, and also the hat had a snake wrapped round the bottom that I think was real.

"That's Osiris, King of the West," said Lauren.

"How do you know?"

"He told me. What did you think?"

I said, "You don't have to snap my head off."

"Well, you always act like you know so much— Like nobody else can know anything."

"Well, sorry!"

"Hunh."

We sat for a while without speaking. But it is

not very comfortable to sit in the dark in a strange place and be fighting with the only person there is to talk to. So I said to Lauren, did she want some candy. We both had some. It was something to do, after all.

But I kept thinking about the guy on the throne, if he really was Osiris. Because I'd read all those library books, or at least looked at the pictures, and the thing is, I actually did know something about Osiris that Lauren didn't know.

"Osiris is the king of dead people," I told her.

"Nuh-uh! He's the King of the West," said Lauren.

"That's just because the west is where the sun goes down. Into the Underworld." I explained to her about Osiris and his boat, the Barque of the Night, that carries the dead person to the Hall of Judgment in the Underworld. I told her about the sarcophaguses and about the book with the hieroglyphics that are supposed to get the dead person safely into the Afterlife. I stood up so that she could see my costume.

"The sarcophagus protects the dead person after he's made into a mummy," I told her. "I think that's where we are, on the Barque of Night."

"Uh, Rachel . . . aren't you forgetting something?"

"Like what?"

"Like, there isn't any dead person."

"Well," I said, hunting around for some kind of tactful way to put it and not finding any, "you are the mummy."

Lauren began to cry. Not real loud, but she just seemed to crumple up like a beachball with no air. I felt awful about it.

I didn't know what to tell her, so I tried changing the subject. That is my mother's advice when things get tense, and sometimes it works. I gave Lauren what was left of the piece of Kleenex my mother used to unsmudge my eye and asked her if she thought Mrs. Vogelman was an alien. I talked about the lunchroom monitors and Larry Spinelli's babysitter, who lets the kids watch gross videos. I asked her if it hurt to have her ears pierced and did she remember that time we made the telephone out of soup cans and string.

"I remember that," said Lauren, smiling just a little. "Those tin-can telephones really work."

"We still have it," I told her. "Danny and Tammy play with it sometimes."

By now we were getting close to the other side

of the river. We could see a big stone building with pillars and torches burning outside and a crowd of more freaky Egyptians on the shore. As soon as the boat got near, some of them ran into the water to pull us up on the bank.

Then Osiris and the others got off the boat one by one and disappeared through the crowd, all except for the dog-face one, who seemed to be waiting for us. I guessed who he was now, jackal-headed Anubis, protector of the dead. I told this to Lauren, who twisted up her face and said, "Oh great."

We got off the boat. Anubis pointed the way to show we were supposed to follow the others. The only thing was, the crowd of Egyptians wouldn't let us through. Every time Lauren and me tried to move ahead, the ones just in front of us would kind of freeze into a wall of mean-looking faces. But the really creepy thing about these guys was, you could only really see them if you were looking right at them. All the others seemed to fade away as soon as you moved your eyes off them a little. I wondered if these were maybe dead people.

"Now what do we do?" I muttered.

"I thought you knew everything," said

Lauren. "I thought you were supposed to protect me."

"The hieroglyphics are supposed to, on the sarcophagus." I touched one of the little pictures with my finger. It felt very warm.

"Ohmigosh, you're glowing!" squeaked Lauren.

"I know it."

"You know so much, what do these guys want, anyway?"

I said I thought they were waiting for some kind of password, like a charm or a prayer or something like what was probably written on my front, in hieroglyphics.

"So why don't you say it, already?" cried Lauren, shaking me by the arm like I'd gone to sleep on the job.

"How am I going to say it?" I shouted back. "You don't think I can read Egyptian, do you? I just copied it out of the book!"

The crowd of ghosts or whatever they were seemed to lean forward at the sound of our voices, like they were moving closer without shifting their feet. Lauren took two quick steps back and got her shoes soaked in the edge of the river.

"Speak the words of power, O Suppliant Soul," commanded Anubis. His voice came out kind of gargled, like a Recorded Announcement.

A little sigh rippled through the crowd, and they drifted nearer. I didn't know any words of power. Alakazam, I thought. Strive for five. Give me liberty, or give me—

"Trickortreat Smellmyfeet Givemesomethinggoodtoeat," said Lauren, real fast.

For one awful, million-year-long moment I thought they were going to rush us. Then the crowd of ghosts swung back, parting in the middle like something painted on the two halves of a double door. Behind them were stone steps leading up to the building with the pillars and torches.

Anubis led the way up the steps. Lauren took one handle of the trick-or-treat bag and I took the other. I couldn't believe how she got away with that smell-my-feet stuff. But one thing about Lauren is, even though she is wrong sometimes, like about the mummy blood, and sometimes she gets in these silly moods, you have to admit she is a quick thinker. I gave her the thumbs-up sign, and she winked back. I didn't know Lauren could wink like that, either.

We followed Anubis into a kind of big shadowy empty hall lined with more pillars that were about as big around as California redwood trees and painted all over with Egyptian pictures. The floor was polished stone that made our footsteps sound lost and lonely. I looked up at the roof. It looked about a mile away.

"I can see stars," whispered Lauren, looking up, too.

In the middle of the hall was a kind of stage, with a stiff-looking throne made out of gold. Osiris was sitting on the throne, and now I saw his face and it wasn't a person face, either. It was a hawk, or maybe an eagle, with huge gold-colored eyes that seemed to stare right through you and out the back of your head at something you didn't know was there yet. Behind him stood two beautiful ladies, or goddesses, I guess they were. They both had long-painted Egyptian eyes and bluey-black Egyptian hair all decorated with gold snakes and jewels and feathers. Also, they had wings, purple-and-black wings that they held out over Osiris. Not angel wings, though. They were more like the wings of a hawk.

The only other thing that we saw in the hall was this humongous balancing scale. The scale was gold and made to look like a tall, skinny woman with her arms stretched out wide. Balancing pans dangled from chains in her hands. Seeing the scale gave me this creepy feeling that all my worst suspicions were about to get proved right.

"Don't worry," said Lauren, giving my arm a little squeeze. "I bet your hieroglyphics will get us out of this okay."

"I bet my hieroglyphics got us into this in the first place! I just wish I knew what I'd wrote."

Anubis went ahead and bowed to King Osiris, and now Osiris was handing him a white feather. I started to explain to Lauren about how that was the Feather of Truth, that Anubis would put on the scale to balance against the heart of the dead person. Because a heart full of bad deeds was supposed to weigh down the scale, but an innocent person's heart was as light as—

"What's that?" hissed Lauren, digging her nails into my arm.

"Ouch, Lauren, leggo my arm!"

"That"—said Lauren, pointing with her head and not letting go of my arm—"*what is that?*"

That was crouched by the base of the scale with its chin between its paws like a dog on a rug. Only it wasn't a dog. To begin with, it was more like a crocodile. But the paws were lion, and so was the curly gold mane that half-hid its mean little crocodile eyes. But not its teeth. The rear part was a big oily black lump ending in stumpy hippopotamus legs.

"It is Ammut the Devourer," said Anubis, pointing with the Feather of Truth.

Ammut grinned at us. That did not make me like him any better.

"Step forward, O Suppliant Soul," said Anubis, cutting the chitchat and getting down to business, "and let us weigh your heart."

He set the white feather in the right-hand pan of the scale. And weirdly the pan rose, as if the Feather of Truth was lighter than the emptiness on the other side.

"Good deeds make light the heart," went on Anubis. "Good deeds are sweet. But evil deeds make the heart bitter and heavy. The heart heavy with bitter deeds must be thrown to Ammut the Devourer."

Ammut got up on his stumpy back legs and his long lion legs and opened his crocodile mouth wide, to show us how much room there was inside.

Lauren made a moaning noise. "Rachel, tell him how he's making a big mistake!"

My first thought, I admit it, was You tell him— I'm going home. Except I didn't know any more than she did how to get there. Then I thought how I'd told Lauren I was the sarcophagus and it was my job to protect her. Besides, she's been my friend practically since kindergarten.

So what I said out loud was "I'm sorry I acted jealous because you won a prize at Handi-Mart."

"It was just pizza coupons," said Lauren.

I asked her if she ever did any good deeds.

"I don't know! I can't think about it with him holding his hand out like that!"

Anubis had stretched out his hand to us. For Lauren's heart.

"Rachel," she wailed, "tell him I'm still using my heart!"

I looked at Anubis. I remembered what he'd said. Good deeds are sweet. I handed Anubis a Milky Way bar. I gave him six Hershey's Kisses and a Mary Jane. One of the Kisses fell on the floor where Ammut the Devourer sniffed at it. He licked his crocodile lips.

I was ladling out candy. Candy corns rained through Anubis's fingers. A mint patty rolled past Ammut. He snapped at it, but Lauren grabbed it first and threw it into the empty pan of the scale. The pan trembled, then lifted a smidgen of an inch off the floor. Both of us piled candy into the pan. It rose some more.

I was starting to sweat. I peeled off my towel headdress and mopped my face.

"Gimme that bag!" yelled Lauren. She lobbed another mint patty behind a pillar. The Devourer galumphed after it.

Lauren threw down the bag. "It's empty!" The candy pan still didn't quite balance with the feather. "What'll we do now?" She clutched my arm.

"Ouch!" cried Lauren, "you're hot!"

It was the hieroglyphics. They were glowing red hot. No wonder I was sweating; all down the front of my costume the gold paint was turning dark. It was like the time my mother overloaded the blender and it smoked and smelled of burned rubber. I was starting to smoke, too.

I tore at the top of the garment bag. "Ow—oww! Get me out of here!"

Lauren found the zipper and tugged. I fell backwards out of my costume and into Lauren's arms as the hieroglyphics burst into a sheet of flame. The flame leaped up with a roar that blotted out everything but its own brightness. Then everything went dark.

The next thing I knew, I was dumped in a heap on a dark, lonely street. I wrapped my arms around myself, because now I was shivering in just my thin clothes.

"I'm going to take a flashlight to bed with me and keep it on all night," said Lauren, behind me in the dark.

I reached around and grabbed a hold of her hand, to help myself up with. Then suddenly I was all right. It wasn't even really very dark. There were porch lights still on. By the door of a house a jack-o'-lantern shone. One half of the jack-o'-lantern's face curved up in a goofy grin. The other half scowled. I was home.

"If you leave it on all night, you'll wear out the batteries," I told Lauren.

"Do you think it's baby?" she asked. "To want the light on?"

"Nooo . . . Not really. But—"

"But what?"

"Flashlights, you know—they kind of jump around, in the dark."

"I know what you mean."

I knew what she meant, too. I wondered if my mother would let me keep the light on in the hall all night. I'd leave my bedroom door open a crack . . . Unless maybe it would be better to lock it. But then it would be dark.

"Uh, Rachel," said Lauren, "you know that old tin-can telephone? You think we could stretch it between our houses tonight? We could talk, you know, in bed."

"Let's go inside and look for it," I told her. "I could use a snack, anyway."

So then I didn't care about the hall light or leaving my bedroom door open anymore. Because it is really a big relief to have your best friend living right next door.

Annie's Pet Witch

WHAT ANNIE MCVITTIE wanted more than anything else was a pet of her own. Annie's pet would not be an ordinary, tame kind of animal. The McVittie family already had a black-and-white cat named Pansyface. Pansyface was a terrific pet for warming toes, or getting rid of any leftover macaroni and cheese. He wasn't much good at games. Annie wanted something with a little wildness left in.

"How about a black panther?" Annie asked her father.

"I can't afford to feed a black panther," said

Mr. McVittie. He shoveled Pansyface off his lap
and reached for the business section of the paper.

"Feed it Pansyface," suggested Annie's
brother, Mark, pulling the Sunday comics out
from under the cat. "There's enough blub on him
to last that panther all winter."

"How about a woolly mammoth?" Annie
asked her mother.

"A woolly mammoth would shed on the furniture," said Mrs. McVittie.

"Hey, listen to this, Dad. This is ace!" said
Mark, reading from the Kids' Pages. " 'There's a
new game on the block and the name is Razor
Wheels. Only $29.95 gives your wheels that le-
thal dose of cool! Plus, you get a—' "

"Okay, then, a boa constrictor," said Annie.
Mark's bike was new, but she was already tired of
it. Besides, he was interrupting.

Mrs. McVittie put down the Neighborhood
News. "When I was a little girl," she said
brightly, "my grandpa taught me how to catch a
wild bunny. All you have to do is tiptoe up behind him—"

"Or her," said Annie.

"Or her," went on Mrs. McVittie, "and sprin-
kle some salt on its tail. The bunny will turn

around to lick up the salt, because little wild creatures can never resist salt. Then you can catch it. Or her."

Annie wasn't sure that bunnies were really wild creatures. Anyway, she did not know if she could catch one, since it was nowhere near Easter. It was almost the end of October. On the other hand, there were plenty of squirrels around that time of year. "I like squirrels," said Annie.

Annie's mother shook her head. She did not think a squirrel would make a good pet.

"I am sure it would bite," she said. But she did not tell Annie no.

Annie made up her mind to catch her new pet right away. She went out the back door, picking up the kitchen salt shaker on the way. The McVitties had a big yard with an oak tree in one corner that was a good place for squirrels. But Annie soon found out that tiptoeing up behind a squirrel is a very difficult thing to do.

Sometimes the squirrels pretended to be too busy to notice her sneaking nearer with the salt shaker, but they always whisked away just in time. So Annie decided to build a trap.

A trap for squirrels is not a very difficult thing to make, if you have a salt shaker and a bag of fresh-roasted peanuts (because squirrels can never resist peanuts), a forked stick, a folding lawn chair, a laundry basket, and plenty of string. Annie had all these things, so of course her trap was a very good one. The squirrels stayed in the oak tree, acting as if they did not care. But Annie could tell they were eager for her to go indoors so they could come down and taste her peanuts.

Annie's mother said it was too late to trap a squirrel that day. "All the little daytime creatures are snuggling into their beds now, Darling. Tomorrow morning we can come out first thing, to look."

. . .

But the next morning Annie found her trap knocked over and her squirrel missing. All she could find were some fat brown toadstools that had nudged their way out of the wet grass.

"Who let my squirrel out?" demanded Annie.

"What makes you think there was ever a squirrel in?" said Mark, kicking the laundry basket out of the way of his bike.

Mrs. McVittie said kindly, "Maybe the little fairies let it go. Wild creatures are supposed to be free."

Then Annie did not mind losing the squirrel. She would much rather have a fairy.

Annie's mother shook her head. She was not sure that a fairy would make a good pet.

"Fairies are very sensitive," she said.

But she did not tell Annie no.

So Annie made a trap for fairies. She tied on the salt and peanuts, just in case, and some brand-new brown toadstools (because fairies can never resist toadstools). Next she set up her forked stick, lawn chair, and laundry basket, and planted tempting flowers all around, in case fairies were sensitive about traps. Then she went indoors to work on her Halloween costume. For the rest of the afternoon she did not visit her trap. Annie knew that fairies would not come out until moonlight.

First thing next morning, Annie hurried out to look. The trap was wrecked, but her fairy had vanished.

"There never was any fairy, you chump!" said Mark, strapping his lunch box and the paper bag with his costume for the middle-school party on the back of his bike.

"It's just what you have to expect, at this time of year," said Annie's mother.

So then Annie knew that Halloween witches must have been there. She was not unhappy. Now that she considered it, a genuine wicked Halloween witch was just the pet she longed for beyond any other. A witch would unlock the secrets of magic for Annie to play with. She might turn her brother's bicycle into a pig.

Annie's mother shook her head. She did not see how a witch could be a pet. A witch would not know how to behave in the house. But she did not tell Annie no.

Annie knew that there is no better time than Halloween night for catching witches. She set to work at once to make her trap strong and sure. She tied on the salt and peanuts and the toadstools, just in case. She left the dead flowers planted all around. Then she got the uneaten half of a macaroni casserole out of the refrigerator. The macaroni was for Pansyface, because witches can *never* resist black cats. Pansyface was black enough at night. Next Annie went to the attic to find the woven-string hammock that her father liked to hang under the oak tree in the summertime. She wrapped the hammock all around her trap and weighted the bottom. It made a net to keep Pansyface from going away, as well as to hold the witch, in case the laundry basket wasn't enough.

It was a long night. The sun was just beginning to squeeze through the gaps in the hedge at the end of the yard when Annie let herself very quietly out of the kitchen door. She could hardly believe what she saw. Something had run—or did it fly?—full tilt into the hammock net, shoving the net into the lawn chair. The force of the shove had snapped the lawn chair shut and driven it clear across the yard, leaving a jet trail of churned-up earth and scattering pieces of the trap along the way. Only, this thing hadn't disappeared, like a jet, over the blue horizon. It was still there, in the lawn chair.

"My witch!"

Annie dove down the back steps and set off across the grass at a run.

There was the witch. Or at least, there were her feet, in raveled black stockings patched with green yarn. Her high-heeled black patent-leather shoes were strapped on with brown-paper package tape, otherwise they would have fallen off, she was kicking so hard. The rest of her was firmly wedged into the collapsed chair. It held her like a giant clam devouring a squid. The hammock heaved. The lawn chair bucked. From inside came the sound of muffled curses.

Annie unwrapped her witch very tenderly. She straightened her legs and her hat, and wiped off macaroni until she was almost as good as new. Annie hoped her witch would be a good sport.

"My name is Annie McVittie," she said politely.

The witch put her face up close to Annie's. She was not very large. She was just tall enough for the brim of her hat to cover them both, like two elves sheltering under a giant toadstool.

"Pleased to meetcha, Bratface," said the witch graciously. "The name is Hagga."

And surely no one could doubt that here was a genuine wicked Halloween witch. But—

"Are you big enough to do magic?" asked Annie.

"Look, Frecklebrain, I ain't no stork. With witches, you got to look at the Nose."

Hagga's nose was something to look at: long, curved, and glowing with the color of moss that grows on the sheltered side of forest trees. Her chin curved up. When she smiled, nose and chin came together like the two parts of a lobster's claw. The witch draped one arm around Annie's shoulders. She was a pretty good sport.

"So, okay, you caught me fair and square," she said. "Now—you got anything to eat around here besides macaroni?"

Mr. and Mrs. McVittie were in the kitchen. Mrs. McVittie was buttering toast.

"Who's your little friend?" she asked Annie.

"She's not my little friend, she's a witch. Her name is Hagga, and I'm going to keep her for a pet."

"Oh, Annie! You know you can't keep a person for a pet." Mrs. McVittie peeked under Hagga's hat. What she saw upset her enough to make her drop the toast on the floor.

"Hagga is not a person," said Annie. "She's a witch."

Annie ate her egg without toast that morning. Hagga ate the eggshells, a jar of instant coffee, and the batteries out of Mr. McVittie's clock radio.

"Witches have iron teeth, see?" She ran her fingernail up and down the rows of teeth. She could play tunes, almost.

"Do you call that music?" cried Mr. McVittie, rushing out the door on his way to work.

"Whatcha expect, 'The Star-Spangled Banner'?" said Hagga.

There was hardly anything worthwhile that Hagga couldn't do. She could turn all the spoon-size Shredded Wheats in Mrs. McVittie's bowl into darling little leaf-brown toads. She could make Pansyface swell up like a balloon and bump gently along the ceiling. Unfortunately, Pansyface got too excited and clawed a lot of things off the china cupboard in the dining room.

By that time Hagga was beginning to yawn. Witches are not used to staying awake during the day. So Annie put her to bed in the dress-up trunk in the attic. Witches prefer places with plenty of dust. Mrs. McVittie didn't leave enough dust for comfort downstairs.

Soon Hagga was snoring loudly. A witch's snores are not like ordinary snores. Sometimes they are loud enough to shiver the floorboards; other times they seem to fade away, then leap out suddenly from unexpected places. Mr. McVittie, home early from his office, spilled half a pot of tea on his best going-to-business trousers when Hagga's snore erupted loudly from the spout.

Witches' dreams are not like ordinary dreams, either. Hagga sent them bowling one by one down the attic stairs. Most of them smashed on the upstairs hall carpet. Some left small sticky puddles, others a peculiar smell. One let loose a cloud of rainbow bubbles that floated all over the house and giggled as they popped. The last dream rolled all the way downstairs and burst with a noise like trucks braking right between Mrs. McVittie's ankles as she was setting supper on the table. Mrs. McVittie dropped the bowl of peas.

Hagga was ready for supper, too. Of course, witches do not care for meat loaf (and not even Pansyface would eat the peas that rolled under the table). Hagga ate half a tin of pepper and the leftover jack-o'-lantern, including the candle stub. She finished off with Mark's left high-top basketball shoe, and spat the gristly bits into the bathroom sink.

Then she was ready for games. She liked Stick-to-the-Ceiling and Rubber Legs. Annie and Hagga practiced shrieking loud enough to make small objects fall off shelves.

"You got to catch 'em by surprise," explained Hagga.

Very soon Mr. and Mrs. McVittie were ready for bedtime. But not Annie.

"Witches stay up all night," she told her mother.

"Then put your witch outside with Pansyface. You will go to bed and stay there until morning."

So Annie put her witch outside. She turned off her light and climbed into bed. She stayed in bed until morning. But the bed did not stay in Annie's bedroom. It tiptoed down the stairs and slipped out through the kitchen door. Annie's bed and Hagga ran races until very late.

When Annie came downstairs the next morning, she saw right away that her family was not happy.

"Annie," said her father seriously, "a witch is not an appropriate pet. A pet is supposed to be an animal."

"A pet should be something cute and lovable," added Mrs. McVittie. "Something to help you learn to be responsible and caring."

"Yeah— Not like Mother Goose goes mutant," stuck in Mark.

"But I caught Hagga all by myself!"

Mrs. McVittie shook her head. And this time she did tell Annie no.

"Your mother and I have agreed to let your witch pass the daylight hours in the attic just for today," said Mr. McVittie. "But when it gets dark, you will have to send her away."

Annie ran upstairs to her room and slammed the door. Annie's mother followed her upstairs. She offered waffles for breakfast and a trip to the shopping mall.

"We could look in the pet store," said Mrs. McVittie, through the keyhole.

Annie put her fingers in her ears. After a while her mother gave up and went downstairs to vacuum the living room.

Annie sat on the floor with her back to the door and her chin on her knees. She was very unhappy. She was also very tired. Annie looked around her room for something quiet to do. Hagga had eaten the hair off her princess doll.

There was a long, jagged tear in the ruffled canopy of Annie's bed, where Hagga had caught her heel, playing Rubber Legs. Then Hagga had tried to change the crayons into colored fireworks, but they had mostly just melted, leaving big smears on the walls and rug. Annie sighed. Maybe a witch was too exciting for every day.

She could hear Hagga snoring up in the attic. Annie opened her door and tiptoed out into the hall. Mrs. McVittie had set a big plastic dishpan at the bottom of the attic stairs to catch the dreams. It was already half full. They looked like little shiny water balloons, different colors.

Annie picked out a dark green one and squinted into it. She thought she could see something inside. She squeezed it. It stretched. All of a sudden it burst, splattering the white paint of the stair rail with green slime. The slime began to ooze down the white rails. As it dripped, it changed into tiny snails with waving eyes that started across the hall carpet and then vanished, gently, in puffs of lime-green steam.

Then Annie noticed the purple dream. It must have missed the dishpan and rolled a little way down the hall. She bent to pick it up. It sparkled pleasantly in her hand. She took the purple dream into her bedroom and held it up to the light from the window. There was something moving inside.

She went up the attic stairs two at a time.

"Hagga, wake up!" Annie shouted over the noise of the snores. She waggled the point of Hagga's shoe where it stuck out over the edge of the dress-up trunk.

Hagga woke up in mid-snore, with a sound like sawing through a violin.

"Listen, Hagga, my parents say I have to let you go."

Hagga opened one eye and glared up at Annie.

"Okay, okay—I get the picture. You want some kind of reward, hunh?" She sounded a little anxious.

"You said I caught you fair and square," Annie reminded her. Even magic has its rules.

Hagga blew through her nose to get out the last of the snores. "I could fix you up a bonzo curse," she suggested.

Annie shook her head. "That's not what I want."

"No gold or jools," grumbled Hagga. "I ain't all that big, you know."

"That's all right," said Annie. "But you can

give me one wish, can't you? Can you give me this?" She held out the beautiful purple dream. "Can you give me what's inside, for my new pet?"

Hagga began to smile. She smiled until the points of her nose and chin met with a click.

"Give it here, Babycheeks," she said, rubbing her hands. "First thing, we got to bring this sucker up to size."

Hagga set the dream on the attic floor. She walked round and round it, muttering spells. Sometimes she did a little footwork, or sang a few lines of a sentimental song. The dream needed lots of encouragement. It grew slowly. It was the size of an orange, then a grapefruit. Hagga's nose had changed from green to fiery red. It looked too hot to touch.

By lunchtime, the dream was the size of a watermelon. Annie could see the creature inside it prancing.

"Oh, how darling!" exclaimed Mrs. McVittie when she came upstairs with a tray of sandwiches and milk for Annie, plus six Brillo pads and a bottle of barbeque sauce with a straw in it for the witch.

By sunset the dream had reached the size of a

baby's blow-up wading pool. It sat on the attic floor and wobbled gently.

"But won't my pet turn into smoke when the bubble pops?" asked Annie.

"Keep your hair on. First we do the charm, then we gotta fix it so it keeps." Hagga thought fiercely. She ground her teeth until they gave off sparks.

"What we need," she said at last, "is a really good shriek."

"I could try," said Annie.

"Naaah— You're good, Stubnose, but you just ain't big enough. What we need is a real Big Mouth."

That gave Annie an idea. "You wait here," she said. "I can fix it."

Annie ran downstairs to the kitchen. Her mother was not there, but her brother, Mark, was spreading jelly on a sandwich.

"Oh, Mark . . ." she said, peering around the edge of the kitchen door. "I'm real sorry . . ."

"Huh?"

"Um, I'm real sorry. For real."

"Sorry about what?" said Mark. "Cough it up."

"I'm real sorry Hagga ate your bike," said Annie, and held her breath.

Hagga was waiting. She caught Mark's shriek neatly as it rose past the attic window. The charm was perfect.

Then it was time for Hagga to go. Annie made her some sandwiches with her mother's Moonglo Blue eyeshadow and Cheez Whiz. She watched as her witch floated away into the nighttime sky, until she looked like no more than a new wart on the chin of the witches' moon. Up in the attic, the purple dream opened like a flower.

The new pet was a great success. It was so cute and lovable that Mrs. McVittie could not say no. It ate only grass, so it was not expensive to feed. And it was very good at games.

Mystery
of the
One-eyed Dog

IT USED TO BE I believed old Captain Sturm was
a pirate. Of course I know it's wrong to judge
people by their appearances, because there's
probably plenty of just ordinary and innocent
ways you could wind up with a black patch over
one eye. Like you could be in a gun battle, or get
blown up by a bomb or something. Only thing is,
Melvin told me— You know that boy Melvin
Reeves, the one goes around telling everybody to
call him the Iceman? He lives the other side of
the fence of Captain Sturm's place. Well, he told
me about how sometimes the Captain'd mow his

grass out back when it's hot, and he'd push that old black patch up on his head the way you do sunglasses. And there was nothing under there but this big red hole!

'Course, you can't just believe everything Melvin Reeves says (I mean the Iceman). Because he is always running his mouth, and it is not serious. Anyway, it just stands to reason a man can't have no great big hole in his head and go on walking around, right? But you know how it is, once you get a hold of a idea like that, it's hard not to think about it.

The other thing about the Captain, he has this big old gray parrot that goes everywhere with him. That bird is better than a dog. Maybe you think a parrot's got to be green or blue or something to be any good, but that just shows how you are ignorant about this subject. Because a African Gray is the smartest bird there is. This parrot rides around on the Captain's shoulder, and sometimes it'll do a little side-steppin' number, nodding its head and spreading out its wings like it was picking up on a beat. Sometimes if the Captain stretch out his arm the bird'll step right down on his finger and *swip!* swing around upside down, laughing.

The truth is, I used to be afraid of that bird. Or maybe not afraid, exactly, but nervous, a little. Because parrots have this trick where they kind of scrape their beaks and make this growly noise. I mean, a bird that size could take your finger off. Maybe it's a surprise the Captain didn't have a ear patch, too, you know what I'm saying?

Which is why, coming home from school, if I'd see the Captain out on his porch I'd go, "Howya doin', Cap'n Sturm?" real polite, and walk fast. See, the way our street is, it's all row houses, stuck together, and the porches are really just one long porch divvied up with little railings. Our mailman can step from porch to porch all the way down the row and swing his leg over the railings. Afternoons, the old folks are mostly sitting out there on the porches. Seems like half of 'em got it in for you, one way or the other.

Like the Captain'd give you this squinty-eye look and that bird let out a cackle. It sounds like a witch. Then maybe Mr. Lewis Tuttle'd tell everybody how he did hate to see healthy young people idling about wasting their time, when he was a boy he had a paper route and made good money, yes sir! Or old Miss Dulcie Dubel, she'd call out, "Why, Kevin Coates, I declare you're skinnier every time I see you! Don't your mama feed you, boy?" Then she'd lean out over her porch rail and holler, "Whyn't you come on in, have a big slice of my homemade coconut cake?"

Miss Dulcie was always making those cakes. It looked like she was made of flour and butter herself, with coconut hair, and always a little round white lacy collar, like you put on a cake plate. Only thing was, nobody'd ever go in Miss Dulcie's house for the cake. Why? 'Cause of the dogs, man. I mean, those dogs were ruthless. At first it was just the one, a black woolly-haired dog like a poodle, only big. And it would bark and growl till it was practically foaming in the mouth if you even just put your foot on the first step of Miss Dulcie's porch. Then she got this bulldog. It was kind of fat and wheezed some and seemed like it was a little lame, too, but a bull's a bull. That kind'll rip you up, anybody knows that.

Miss Dulcie went on offering everybody the cake, even though couldn't nobody get near it. She used to pester the life out of old Mr. Bunce, that lived in Captain Sturm's house before the Captain, and he was already so fat he'd got to lean on a cane to walk. Then Mr. Bunce went away kind of sudden, I never did hear exactly why, and Captain Sturm moved in. He used to say, "No thank you, Miss Dubel, I don't eat much sweets." And those dogs snarling away like they'd eat *him*, and not wait for a napkin, either.

Well, that's how things were until Halloween come around. I was fixing to get out round the old 'hood with my posse—that's the Iceman and Danny G. and Rick Biggles and me. I was a pirate. Because mostly we go for the candy anymore, but you got to dude yourself up some or they don't give out.

And this time my costume was really fresh, 'cause my sister Celia lended me this totally cool piece of phony hair she bought to go to a dance, only she didn't have the nerve to wear it, for a chin beard. I mean, *I* wore it for a chin beard. My sister was supposed to put it on her head.

We did pretty good and just about stuffed ourselfs with Mars bars and junk. And some of the ones Danny couldn't eat, 'cause he's allergic, we put in the street and stomped on. It was a real wicked night, with the wind rushing through the dark, and half the time the moon shining and making big shadows and half the time black as my you-know-what, and this cold wind grabbing the back of your neck like skeleton fingers.

So when we got to Melvin's house, Mrs. Reeves gave us cocoa, and Rick, he said he didn't want to go round no more.

Then the Iceman says to me, "Dare you to look in old man Sturm's windows."

And Rick goes, "What'd he want to do that for, man?"

"Bet you he takes that patch off, indoors," says the Iceman. "Then you'd see that big old red hole."

So I go, "Who you tryin' to put that big lie on, man? You know he don't have no red hole."

But he just goes, "Dare you."

Well, we could see the lights shining across the back yard from the Captain's kitchen. There was a fence, but it wasn't anything but a bit of old chicken wire. I was real quiet. Seemed like, away from the lighted windows, it was extra dark on Halloween night.

Nobody in the kitchen. I saw the kitchen table laid out for the Captain's supper. I couldn't get to the dining-room windows without climbing up on a trash can. Nobody in there, either. I was kind of reaching up on tiptoe, standing on the can lid so's I could see on into the living room, when *bang! crang!* the can went over. *Hooooo,* man! It made a racket like the end of the world. Then *whump!* these great big heavy CLAWS grabbed me from behind!

I about died right there. If I yelled, it wasn't any more than you would of done. Man, I was out of there so fast—I felt the claws drop off me and heard this crazy witchy cackle, and I was hightailing it over the fence and back to old Melvin's. Melvin'd left a light on over the kitchen door for me. I'd just about made it, too, when WHUMP! Those claws digging in my back again! I'm telling you, man, felt like all my blood jumped down to my toes, and my heart going whumpa-whumpa and my legs just fell out from under my stomach.

I turned my head real easy. The first thing, I saw this big, hooky beak, right up near my eye. It was the Captain's parrot that was landed on my shoulder, with its claws digging in to hold on by.

I scrunched my shoulder up and down a few times and went, Shoo.

The parrot only wobbled a bit and ruffed its feathers. It came to me like that bird didn't belong to be outside, not cold like it was, and windy, too. Then it leaned over with its beak and kind of tasted my pirate beard, real gentle. And

you know something? A parrot's got a tongue looks just like people's. It's a funny thing, I never exactly noticed before that birds have tongues.

I said, "Hey, little guy—what you doin' out all by yourself?"

Actually, that parrot's supposed to be a female, and her name is Dot, but I didn't know that then. She didn't answer, either. Come to mention it, I didn't ever hear that bird talk before.

Well, I was feeling pretty teed with Melvin for setting me up for a shock like he did, so I decided he could just wait and wonder while I cut back to my street through the little alley runs next to Miss Dulcie's. I didn't figure I ought to be knocking on the Captain's back door, not that time of night. But he didn't answer at his front door, either. The porch was dark. I knocked and rang for a long time, in case he didn't hear me over the racket Miss Dulcie's dogs were making.

Miss Dulcie opened her door and talked to me through the screen. She told me the Captain'd gone away.

"Gone where?" I said. I thought she meant to the 7-Eleven or something.

"I really couldn't say," she told me. "Seems like he was called away sudden."

"Well, when's he going to come back, then?"

"I really couldn't say, dear." She was looking at me like I was supposed to say good night now, but I didn't, so she went on, "I expect he'll write us a postcard. Good night, dear."

"But, Miss Dulcie, he couldn't just *go away* and leave his lights on and everything!"

"Oh dear . . . How careless."

"Look," I said, "I got his bird."

"His bird?" she said, looking at me kind of blank. "Well—I'm sure the Captain'll be mighty grateful to you for looking after his pet." She sparkled at me a little with the rhinestones in her glasses frames, like sugar. "That's real sweet of you, Kevin honey. I'm sure he'll thank you when I get a postcard from him tomorrow. Good night, now."

She was shutting her door. She didn't even offer me any trick or treat.

"Miss Dulcie, wait!" I rattled the screen. "What'm I supposed to do—"

But her door was shut tight. I could see her through the glass, standing in her front hall. And you know something? There were *three dogs* in there with her! The black, and the fat bull, and a new red-haired, skinny little guy that throwed himself against that door and barked till I thought he'd shake his chin whiskers off.

The Captain still hadn't got home the next day after school when I went to take back his bird. I rang the front doorbell till my finger near about dropped off, then went round the back and knocked at the kitchen, but he didn't answer there, either. So then I didn't know what to do.

Whiles we were waiting out there in the Captain's yard I shared a Fifth Avenue bar out of the trick or treats with the parrot. I hope that wasn't wrong, because she seemed to like it okay. She'd ruffed up her feathers and was making that scrapy, growly noise with her beak. Only this time I thought it sounded kind of friendly, almost like purring. I tried tickling her on the top of the head, and she liked that, too. Her feathers are all tipped in black, layer over layer like fish scales, only soft and warm. I wished my mom wouldn't of made me take her back.

All of a sudden the parrot slicked down her feathers and sat up sharp. It was Miss Dulcie, come out on her kitchen porch, that startled her.

Miss Dulcie went, "Why, it's Kevin! What you doing out there, dear?" Just like she didn't practically slam the door on my nose the night before.

I said, "How you doin', Miss Dulcie. I was wondering, did you hear from Captain Sturm today at all?"

But she just laughed, so the flour fell off her apron and her glasses bumped up on top of her nose.

"Whyn't you come on in the kitchen, Kevin, have a big slice of my coconut cake? Just made fresh this morning."

I said no, thank you, ma'am, maybe I was allergic to coconut.

But she goes, "Now, don't let those itty-bitty little old dogs trouble a big boy like you. They are all taking a nice nap in my back parlor." (She meant the dining room. All those houses on our street laid out the same.) "I'll just close the kitchen door, and you'll be fine."

So I said okay. Because I had a suspicion she knew more about the Captain's disappearance than what she said last night. I was thinking, number one, maybe I could get it out of her, what she was trying to hide. And number two, I'm not actually allergic to coconut.

Well, right away it turned out Miss Dulcie hadn't been exactly straight with me, because that door in the kitchen was only half a door. I mean, the bottom half of it was shut all right, but the top hung open on its own. Those dogs weren't napping, either. They commenced to jump and howl.

The little red dog and the bull were too short-legged to get over the door. The black one got his paws right up and looked like he was coming over the top. But Miss Dulcie, she took a hold of her cake slicer and *whap!* She let that woolly-headed pooch have it right between the ears with the china handle end. The dog slunk down on the floor, and the other two dogs slunk down, rolling their eyes, and whining and growling all together.

"Watch your step, Preeble!" snaps Miss Dulcie, sounding flat-out mean.

Seemed to me then that it was a funny thing she kept so many dogs if she didn't like them any better than that.

The parrot, she was still perched on my arm, and she stuck out her neck and bust loose a *word*—it was the first time I ever heard that bird talk. Miss Dulcie spun around and leveled at us with the cake slicer. She wasn't used to that kind of language, I guess. You could practically see the smoke curling out of her ears.

Miss Dulcie goes, "Get that dirty bird out of my kitchen," spitting out the words with tight lips like you do watermelon seeds, if you want them to really sting when they hit. The parrot had got her wings spread out and her head pushed forward like the American eagle on the post-office trucks. Miss Dulcie flapped her cake slicer. "Shoo! Get away from here!"

The bird took off then, swooping low over Miss Dulcie's head. Miss Dulcie ducked. Then *swoop*, through the open top of the half-door, and landed smack on the back of the little red dog!

I bet you think it scared the hair off of him, right? But no way; the dog reached his head around and tried to give that bird a lick, nice and gentle, like they were old friends. And that's when I saw it. That dog had just the one eye! I didn't notice how it was at first, because the other eye was just closed, like naturally— You wouldn't hardly tell there was anything the matter with it. But it didn't open up at all.

I was starting to have my suspicions. And what I suspicioned was, how come every time some old guy disappears around here Miss Dulcie winds up with a new dog? Because I don't know where

the old black poodly one come from, but I remember when she got the bull. And it was right
when Mr. Bunce went away.

Miss Dulcie had her mouth hanging open—I
guess we both did—but she got a hold of herself
and shut hers so's I could hear the teeth click.
After a minute she says, "Why, Kevin dear,
you're still waiting on that cake."

She slapped a fat chunk on a china plate and
set it on the kitchen table for me. It did look
seriously tasty.

Then she goes, "Lemonade?"

And I go, Yes, ma'am, just like I never had any
suspicions at all. But all the time I was stretching
my neck trying to keep an eye on my bird, and
that little red one-eye dog.

Miss Dulcie didn't cut any cake for herself, either. I asked her didn't she want some, but she
didn't seem to hear. Instead, she acted busy at
the sink with the cake slicer. I don't mean she
washed it off, like my mom would of done. She
just set it in the sink in this real finky way, like
she was too delicate to touch dirty dishes or
something. Which maybe she was, 'cause there
was a whole load of them in the sink, which surprised me for a fussy lady like Miss Dulcie.

"Mrs. Coombs will come in the morning and wash up," she said, like she could see what I was thinking, so I felt kind of embarrassed.

I said, "I see you got a new dog, Miss Dulcie. What's his name?"

"Captain," she said, coming over to sit with me at the table. "How's that cake?"

"Oh, fine. Fine. How about the other two? What you call them?"

"The black one's Mr. Preeble. And I call the bulldog Roscoe."

I could tell she had her eye on my clean fork. "Great cake," I said, mashing it up some. But I'd made up my mind, there was no way I was going to actually eat that cake. Because here she was, shoving it in everybody's face, then acting like she couldn't even touch one little crumb of it herself. Stands to reason there must be something funny about it, right?

Miss Dulcie gave me a real sweet smile and said, "How you like school this year, Kevin?"

So I told her, "Shoot, I don't see much point of school, Miss Dulcie. I'm just hanging in there till I'm old enough to quit."

I don't want you to believe I meant that for serious. The thing is, I've noticed that quitting school is one subject that's a hundred percent guaranteed to keep any adult person gabbing for as long as you want to keep them at it. The fact is, I was beginning to feel nervous about Miss Dulcie.

It came to me like she might be some kind of a witch. I tried to remember anything I ever learned about witches, but I could only think of dumb stuff like Halloween songs we had to learn in school. I always hated those, where you have to pretend you're a pumpkin or something and go woo-woo like a total fool. I saw *The Wizard of Oz* on TV. There was a Wicked Witch of the West in that.

So whiles Miss Dulcie was jib-jabbering away about my education, I just leaned forward, with my glass of lemonade in my hand, making out like I was listening so hard I'd forgot all about eating. But all the time I was trying to remember what happened to that Wicked Witch of the West. I'm not saying like I believed in any Oz or like that, only when the going gets rough you can't just sit around, let the other guy make all the moves. You got to be the man with the plan.

"So now you won't talk any more about letting go of your precious opportunity for an education, will you, dear?'' says Miss Dulcie, wrapping it up.

"No, ma'am." And I leaned forward a little more, like I had to scratch my ankle or something, only I'd still got the glass in my hand, see?

Then Miss Dulcie goes, sounding real sharp, *"Why don't you eat that cake?"*

Man, I jumped. And the lemonade, it like slooped out of the glass. I figure some of it must of fell on Miss Dulcie's shoe, under the table there.

Because you never saw nothing like it, man— that shoe was *smoking*. And Miss Dulcie, she was hollering and jumping round like she was on fire. Then in the other room all the dogs got to jumping round, too, going WUWUWUWUWUWUWUH! And the parrot was screeching worse than Miss Dulcie, even.

Miss Dulcie got the shoe kicked off, which was no cinch, since it was one of those lace-up-to-the-ankle kind old ladies wear a lot of. That shoe laid there on the kitchen floor, with the toe all curled up and sizzling. Then Miss Dulcie, she got her back up against the fridge and she goes, "Don't do it!" Like this was some kind of stickup and I was holding a .38 police special instead of a dumb old glass of lemonade.

I expect by now you remembered, too, how Dorothy melted the Wicked Witch of the West.

I said, "Miss Dulcie, the game's up."

You could tell she didn't like it much. I'll tell it to you raw and real, man, she was mad enough to bite. But I just took a stroll over to the sink and turned the taps on, hard. It was better than I expected. The water hit the cake slicer and splattered out all over the room. I got soaked.

Miss Dulcie screeched, "Don't do that! I'll let 'em go—just leave them taps alone!"

"I'm watching you," I told her. "Better get a move on or I'll melt you."

I know that's no way to talk to a lady, but the way I figured it, Miss Dulcie was really more like a criminal.

Miss Dulcie opened the other half of the parlor door and walked through, whipping back a few mean looks at me as she went. I followed her, carrying a dirty cake pan I found in the sink, filled with water. The dogs were all scrunched down around her feet whining and squirming, you know the way they do, with their tails going whap-whap! back and forth on the carpet. All except for the bull, that didn't hardly have any tail to speak of and had to wag his whole hind end. The parrot was still hanging on to the little one-eye dog, and it got wagged with the rest.

Miss Dulcie really surprised me. Well, she'd been doing that right along, I guess, but now she commenced to strutting and prancing around with her finger in the air, rapping her stuff. She was heavy on her legs for that kind of action, but if her rhythm was missing, her power was right on.

"Getcher tails twitchin'," rapped Miss Dulcie. "Hang your ears down low— Get ready for the power 'cause it's ready to blow!"

The dogs were howling, *Owoooo-oo!* There was something happening, that's for sure, 'cause the room was full of smoke.

"Getbackgetbackgetback, keep your body low— Better *get back!*"

I could hear the dogs sneezing like firecrackers going off and see Miss Dulcie's finger whipping round, stirring up the smoke. The smoke made me want to rub my eyes something bad, but there was no way I was going to let go of that pan of water.

"Respect the power!" sang out Miss Dulcie, " 'cause it's READY TO BLOW!"

"OWOWOW-OOOO!"

Then Miss Dulcie leveled her finger at Mr. Preeble like she was planning to blow him away with it and said, "Do it!"

There was a flash like a instant camera going off and the smell of burned coconut. And the dog was gone, man! Instead, there was humped up on the rug this long, lean old brother in a gray mailman's suit.

Next she did her number on the bulldog. "*Do it!*" Flash! Sizzle! And it's Mr. Bunce, just like I suspicioned.

Last of all, she got to the Captain. When she stuck her finger at the one-eye dog, the parrot took a swipe at it with her beak open.

"*Do IT!*" squawked Miss Dulcie. Sure enough, there was Captain Sturm, with the parrot still hanging on to his back.

Miss Dulcie was sucking her finger. She quit prancing and blew her nose and waved at the smoke with a little hankie that had pink daisies stitched on it.

And there were those three old guys facedown on the parlor carpet, with their you-know-whats up in the air, wagging fit to bust a bootlace.

Mr. Preeble was the first to get up. He put his hand to the back of his neck and cracked his joints and said, "Lord help me, feels good to set up straight!"

Then he went over and jogged Mr. Bunce's elbow and helped him get up on his feet.

Mr. Bunce said, "Where the blankety-blank did that woman put my cane?"

The parrot nipped Captain Sturm on his ear, not in a mean way. He got up, too, and scratched his chin beard. He didn't look like a pirate then, just like a old man woke up too sudden. The one eye was closed, perfectly naturally, so you wouldn't hardly notice it was blind.

Miss Dulcie gave us all a long look to let us know she wished we'd dry up like spit on a griddle. But what she said was "Now if you gentlemen will excuse me, I think I'll go lie down for a while."

Mr. Preeble said, "Certainly, ma'am," and we all filed out on the front porch. Only first I had to find a good place to set down my pan of water. I settled for the top of the parlor door, 'cause I didn't trust that Miss Dulcie Dubel.

The mailman, his name was Mr. Elton Preeble, apologized to me for barking and carrying on like he did. He was only trying to keep me away from that cake, he said. I explained to everybody about how Dorothy throwed the bucket of water on the Witch of the West. And they all said I was pretty smart to think of that. Then Mr. Preeble shook hands all around and said he'd better be getting home 'cause his wife would be wondering. I never did see him after that time. But my mom said, sure she remembered Mr. Preeble, he must of retired years ago, he was that old. So probably that's what he did do.

I got to be good friends with Captain Sturm. And Mr. Bunce, too. Since they'd both rented the same house, they decided to live there together. The Captain lets me hold Dot, the parrot. I'm teaching her to talk. She can already say a bunch of stuff: "Yo, Brother!" and "What's happenin' " and "Take it easy, Roscoe." Turns out she's only a young bird, so it stands to reason she didn't learn before. 'Cause when was she going to get the chance to hear the Captain talk, living alone like he did?

And you know something else? You probably guessed the Captain wasn't any pirate. Turns out, he never even was on a boat except one time a paddleboat down at the harbor. Captain Sturm is a ex-policeman.

Me and Mr. Bunce wanted him to march right over and arrest that Miss Dulcie.

"That woman's a menace, Joe," says Mr. Bunce, biting down on his cigar end.

The Captain tries to scratch his beard with his foot. (He told me that was a habit he picked up easy as a dog and couldn't lay down now he'd switched back.) "Well, I don't know," he goes, squinting like he always does when he's feeling shy. "What'd I charge her with, you tell me that. What's the charge?"

"Get 'er with a cake and battery!" hollers Mr. Bunce, banging on the table.

Then he laughs so hard he wheezes and turns purple and his cigar rolls under his chair. Captain Sturm has to pound him on the back. "Take it easy, Roscoe."

Only he never did get to arrest Miss Dulcie. She didn't answer at the front door when we knocked, and the kitchen was too full of smoke to see in at the back windows. There's a sign on Miss Dulcie's house now, says FOR SALE. So maybe she just moved away real sudden. Which is why, if your folks tell you don't take sweets from strangers, you better listen up, they might know more about it than what you think. Because I don't know where Miss Dulcie Dubel is moved to.

The Paper Bag Genie

MRS. POLSKI SAID, "I never saw nothing like this weather for wind! You're liable to catch your death out there on the street, Jewel."

Jewel was sitting at the kitchen table with her head propped on her hand. Her freckled elbow and the fall of her hair made a screen to block her grandmother's view of her plate. Now she sat up straight and took her elbows off the table.

"It's just *wind*, Mommom," she said. "You don't mean I got to stay home on Halloween."

Mrs. Polski said, "You eat your dinner, maybe you can go on over Gruber's Shopping Center.

Since they got that roof put up over the middle, you don't hardly notice the weather or nothing."

"Mommom, nobody calls it Gruber's anymore," said Jewel's sister, Ashley. "It's the Mall."

"So what'm I supposed to do there?" said Jewel.

"For crying out loud, Jewel," said Ashley, "they got stores, don't they? You're supposed to trick-or-treat 'em, dumbo."

"Trick or treat at the Mall?" Jewel plonked her fork down on the metal top of the table. "That's for babies!"

Mommom knocked her cigarette ash against the rim of her saucer. She said, "Ashley'll walk you over, hon. You know I can't go out there in that wind. My authoritis's liable to set up solid."

"I don't want her tagging along with me the whole time," Ashley complained. "Sharon and me've got plans."

Mommom rolled her eyes up at the ceiling. That was her way of saying when Ashley and Jewel were out of line. She always told those girls she couldn't stand to think their mamma would look down from heaven and see them acting ignorant. Then Mommom stubbed out her cigarette and leveled with Ashley. "Ashley," she said, "I don't see how you expect to get a nice complexion if you don't eat your greens."

Ashley and Jewel and Ashley's friend Sharon cut across the parking lot to the Mall. Jewel walked tiptoe in the wind. She could feel it trying to lift her up, to whirl her away over the parked cars and the flat roof of the Mall.

Jewel was Wonder Woman. She had the shiny cape and smiling face mask that had been Ashley's when she was in third grade. Mommom said she wasn't paying the kind of money they were asking nowadays for those horrible rubber things when the Wonder Woman only needed new elastic. The inside of the mask felt sticky from Jewel's breathing. But the good thing about Wonder Woman, thought Jewel, was that she could fly. Jewel stretched out her arms to the wind.

Lightning glimmered in the sky. It was followed by a sudden loud tearing noise and a gust of wind that stung Jewel's legs with grit from the pavement.

"Run for it!" yelled Ashley, racing ahead. Sharon followed her.

"You guys—watch out—" panted Jewel, far behind. "Car coming!"

The girls turned to look, but there was no car, only a paper bag puffed up like a balloon and twisted shut at the top. It made a surprising lot of noise blowing and scraping across the parking lot.

Ashley clasped her hands and rolled up her eyes. "Oh, please don't let my poor little baby sister get run over," she prayed.

"It's just trash," said Sharon.

"Splat! Death by deli bag," shouted Ashley. "Come on, Sharon!"

Jewel trotted after the two big girls. She could hear the bag rushing after her.

"Ashley, wait up— I got a funny feeling— You know, about that bag?—"

Ashley waited. "What kind of feeling?"

"Just . . . funny."

"Ha ha."

"No, I mean like a weird feeling. It's still following us."

"Listen, Jewel, that is about the dumbest thing you ever said in your whole life. How can a bag be following us?"

The three girls turned to look at the bag again.

It was closer than before. They could see red lettering across the front: SOLLY'S EASTERN CARRY-OUT, and a splot of mustard.

"Stomp on it," said Sharon.

Jewel didn't want to.

Ashley said, "I know what's in there." She lowered her voice and opened her eyes wide, wide, with the white showing all around the blue. "It's a cut-off head. You could make the front page: GIRL KICKS PAPER BAG, OUT POPS MAN'S HEAD."

"Gross!" shrieked Sharon.

"That's why they're called head-lines, get it?"

Sharon didn't. "Can't you guys hurry up?" she said. "My hair's getting all ruined."

Ashley and Sharon linked arms and ran, bumping and staggering because Ashley was taller. By the entrance to the Mall they turned and looked back at Jewel. Ashley did a crazy face, crossing her eyes and making cuckoo circles with her fingers.

"Don't talk to any strange paper bags," she hollered.

Jewel glared at the deli bag. "Dumb old bag."

The bag came skittering to her feet as if she'd whistled for it. Jewel took a quick backward step.

"I could stomp on it if I want to."

"I would not advise you to do so, however," said a voice. It was a small, dry, papery voice. It sounded almost as if it came from the paper bag.

Jewel turned all the way around in a circle. There was no one near. Ashley and Sharon had disappeared into the Mall.

"She's not supposed to leave me all by myself where there's cars," said Jewel to herself. "I'm going to tell Mommom this is all her fault."

"Speak up," said the bag, "don't mumble! I can't hear a word you're saying with this paper rustling in my ears."

"Uh," said Jewel. She wondered if talking to paper bags proved you were crazy. On the other hand, she didn't like to act rude to some-body who might turn out to be a cut-off head. She tried again. "Uh . . . you mind if I ask, are you a, uh . . . ?"

"I am a genie," said the voice in the bag.

"You mean, like Aladdin and the, uh . . . ?"

The bag wheezed and puffed up. "Behold!" it crackled. "Behold, *I am he who consumes the earth with tongues of fire.*"

"Oh! I mean, uh . . . I'm Jewel."

"A beautiful name," replied the bag.

"Hunh!" said Jewel. "How'd you like to have a name rhymes with drool? You want to hear a awesome name, my sister's name is Ashley."

"I prefer Jewels to Ashes," said the voice in the bag.

Jewel pushed the Wonder Woman mask up on her head. The mask smiled blank-eyed at the sky, and Jewel smiled at the deli bag. "I didn't mean to interrupt," she said.

The bag made a crumpling noise like a paper throat being cleared. "The wind is my mantle and the stars my crown," it intoned. "In my left hand I grip the thunderbolt, and with my right pour out the riches of the earth!"

Even the wind seemed to hush respectfully. A slim moon broke through the clouds and shone down on the parking lot. Jewel took a deep breath.

"The thing I don't understand," she said, "if you're a genie, how come you're not in a bottle?"

At once the moon vanished. The bag began to rock in the wind. Sighs whistled through the neck of the bag, and damp spots appeared on the paper.

"I didn't mean nothing bad," cried Jewel. "You need a Kleenex? I got some—"

"Thank you," replied the voice thickly. "I have a paper napkin."

The bag gave out a series of rolling honks that were echoed in the sky by a drumroll of thunder.

"Did you see that?" said the voice, sounding suddenly more cheerful.

"What?"

"The lightning! To tell the truth, it's been quite some time since I did much Consuming the Earth. Nice to know I haven't lost my touch, eh?"

"You mean you did that?"

The bag remained modestly silent.

"Oh wow," said Jewel, "what else can you do? Can you fly? Can you— I mean, do you think you could—make *me* fly?"

"That depends . . ." said the voice in the bag.

"Depends on what?"

"It depends," said the genie, "on the bottle. Allow me to tell you my story."

The genie's story was short but tragic. There had once been a time when he did have a bottle. A proper magical bottle, he told Jewel, stamped with the seal of King Solomon, wisest of mortals and most potent of magicians. After a glamorous career in the lands of the fabled East, the bottle came to America, tucked in a shipment of Greek olives. There it was found by the owner of Solly's Eastern Carryout, Mrs. Mahmuzlu Camgöz.

"Mamma Zl—who?"

"I arrived," said the genie, ignoring Jewel's interruption, "as the fulfillment of that lady's wildest dreams. But alas, Mrs. Camgöz is a person totally without imagination. Her wildest dream was for somebody to wash the dishes and sweep the floors without pay."

So, week after week, year after year, the miserable genie washed and swept. Meanwhile, the precious bottle sat on the counter between the cash register and a stack of carryout menus. Mrs. Camgöz had filled it with toothpicks.

"You ought to take it back from her!" said Jewel.

"Alas!" cried the voice of the genie, and all around the parking lot the wind heaved a great sigh. Three drops of rain fell and rattled the mask on Jewel's head.

The genie wept. "I have the soul of an artist. I might have built her palaces of porphyry, gardens of lotus and rose. But what did she want? Slop buckets!"

Rain splotched the shiny Wonder Woman cape. Jewel shook her head—too bad. Then she wondered if he could even see, inside that bag.

"Oh, I tried to escape," continued the genie, with a sob in his voice. "I hid in a carryout bag. The man—who ordered the sandwich—said—'I wish I'd remembered to order extra onions—' He wished it, and I couldn't do it!" The bag let out a despairing wail. "I couldn't—produce—an onion!"

"You mean," said Jewel flatly, "you're supposed to give wishes but you can't?"

"You must help me! I knew at once, from your heroic garb, you were the one—"

Jewel fingered her Wonder Woman cape. Underneath she wore Ashley's old baton twirler's skirt and a T-shirt that said *WMOO Country.*

"You must go to Solly's Carryout and rescue my bottle!" declared the genie.

"You mean, just go in there and grab it off the counter?" Jewel gnawed her lip. She hated to let down the only person who had ever called her heroic. "I think that's maybe shoplifting," she said.

"Then I am doomed," sighed the bag.

"Listen, I'm real sorry—"

"Doomed . . . to wander alone, friendless and discarded . . . a scrap of trash in an empty parking lot—"

"You don't understand, a person can go to jail for that."

"O desert night, milky with stars," cried the genie, "when shall I again behold you? When shall I see the black shadow of a carpet sliding over the moon-silvered dunes?"

Jewel gulped. "You could do that? A magic, uh, a *flying* carpet?"

"Of course," said the genie, sounding suddenly quite businesslike. "Though many of my masters have preferred a train of five hundred camels with their attendants. A very distinguished mode of travel, I feel. Or if you're in a hurry, you might try seven-league boots— Though I don't personally recommend the boots. It is difficult to see in advance where one will step."

"Oh yeah, I know what you mean," said Jewel eagerly. "One time I was running on the beach, I stepped on this old bait fish, pee-ew! And—uh— what I mean is, maybe we could just go have a talk with this Mrs.—uh, Camguts— Maybe—"

Lightning blazed across the sky. The rest of Jewel's words were swallowed up in a roar of thunder. Rain spattered the paper bag. The bag trembled all over and scooted to shelter between Jewel's feet.

"Help me," whimpered He Who Consumes the Earth with Tongues of Fire.

The Mall smelled of popcorn and fry oil and new shoes. Jewel, with the genie's bag hidden under her cape, cruised the food area. Taco Tico—Pizzarama—Olde Worlde Deli Sandwiches. She didn't see any Solly's. She didn't see Ashley and Sharon, either.

"You'd think she'd of at least waited around to check if I got here okay," grumbled Jewel.

"Hush!" hissed the voice in the bag. "Do not call the notice of the crowd to me by speaking."

"What crowd?" said Jewel.

A man behind the counter at Sushi Shack smiled at Jewel. "Not many trick-or-treaters made it out in this weather," he said.

Jewel went over and held the deli bag up for him to see. "Uh, excuse me—can you tell me—"

The counterman took the bag from Jewel. He opened the top and dropped in a double handful of Big Gob purple gumballs. A breath of smoke puffed out of the open top.

"Neat trick," said the man politely, handing the bag back to Jewel.

Jewel clutched it shut. "Ohmigosh, are you okay in there?" she hissed.

"Beg pardon?" said the counterman.

Jewel held the bag tight, out of his reach. "You know where I can find this place, Solly's?" she asked him.

He pointed down the corridor, past the rest-rooms, past the telephones and the utility area where the janitors kept their buckets and brooms.

"But I don't think you'll like their food," he told her.

"Why not?"

The man shrugged. "It's foreign," he said.

Jewel's footsteps sounded loud in the empty corridor. "Is it okay if I take a piece of gum?" she asked.

"Shh!"

"Listen," she said to the genie, "nobody's around here. We can talk loud as we want."

"Mahmuzlu Camgöz has very sharp ears," mumbled the voice in the bag.

"Well, so, can I open this bag? I want to look inside."

"Certainly not!" squawked the voice. "I am

twenty-two feet tall, and my eyes are orbits of fire. You have no respect."

"Don't be mad. I just wanted to see how you fit—"

"I fit where I please," said the genie, "and I appear as I please. But you despise me because I have no bottle."

"Look, don't take it like that," begged Jewel. "I'm trying to help you, aren't I? Just please don't cry anymore."

"I am not crying."

"Your voice sounds all funny."

"I am chewing gum," said the genie.

Jewel took off her cape and wrapped it around the bag before she went into the restaurant. She found Mrs. Camgöz waiting for her behind the carryout counter.

"What you want, hon?" she said.

Then Jewel felt the spit drying up in her mouth. Mrs. Camgöz had the air and figure of a Saturday-morning TV wrestler. She wore a gray athletic T-shirt with GOVERNMENT ISSUE stamped across the front. Her hair was the color of canned peaches. But it was her eyes that fascinated Jewel.

Mrs. Camgöz had one eye the color of cold lentil soup. The other—round, bland, and baby-blue—stared off at an odd angle, as if its job were to look around the back of Jewel while the lentil eye sized up the front.

With an effort Jewel dragged her gaze away from the baby-doll-blue eye. She saw there wasn't any bottle on the counter. There was nothing at all on the counter but Mrs. Camgöz's elbows.

"You want something or not?" said Mrs. Camgöz. She breathed heavily through her mouth when she spoke.

"French fries!" squeaked Jewel. "I mean, uh, small order of fries, please. Lots of ketchup."

"Ketchup is extra," said Mrs. Camgöz.

"That's okay," said Jewel, fingering the coins in her skirt pocket. "I mean, uh, just the french fries, please."

The fries were cool and smelled fishy. Jewel held on to them like an admission ticket as she wandered around the tiny room. She saw no place to hide a bottle, except— A curtain of plastic beads covered the entrance to an inner room. Jewel lifted a strand of beads to peer in.

"You mind if I eat in there?" she asked.

"The Acropolis Dining Room is only if you order dinner," said Mrs. Camgöz.

Jewel pretended to study a travel poster on the wall. She hugged the bundled cape with the genie's bag to her side, away from Mrs. Camgöz's eyes.

"Now what do I do?" she muttered, trying to talk out the side of her mouth. There was no answer.

"You don't expect me to order dinner, do you?" she said. "I just spent all my money. Anyways, I already had my dinner."

The genie's voice was so soft it seemed to come from inside her own head. "Order fish," it said.

Jewel stared at the travel poster. Either the picture was very faded or the lady in the bathing suit was very cold, because her skin was the same color blue as the lake behind her. BEAUTIFUL BALUCHISTAN, read the caption. Jewel turned and gave Mrs. Camgöz a beautiful smile. Inside, she felt as cold as lakewater.

"I decided to order dinner," she said.

Mrs. Camgöz led the way into the Acropolis Dining Room. She moved very quietly for a woman her size, as if she rolled on little wheels like a piano. The room was long and dim. Nobody else was eating in there. For decoration there were loops of fish netting hung from the ceiling, tangled with beachcombers' junk, dried starfish and cork floats, bottles and plastic trout. It made Jewel think of the Jaycees' Haunted House in the school gym. Any minute she expected Mrs. Camgöz to produce a plate of cold spaghetti and tell her it was dead men's guts.

Mrs. Camgöz slapped a menu down on one of the empty tables. All of the tables were empty, except for Jewel's. One side of the menu listed American Food: Cheeze Sandwich, Fruit Cocktail. There was nothing that would take time to prepare, nothing to give Jewel time to search. The other side listed Eastern Delicasies. Jewel's finger traveled along the unfamiliar words, Skuše Marinirane, Tunj Kao Pašticada, Sayadieh. She certainly wasn't going to order fish. Jewel hated fish.

"Well?" said Mrs. Camgöz, breathing hard.

Jewel poked her finger down blindly on the menu. "This one," she said. It was Ochtapódi Krassáto, and it cost fifteen dollars. "Is that fish?" she asked.

"Everything is fish," said Mrs. Camgöz darkly, taking back the menu. On her way out to the kitchen she turned around once to say, "I smell gum. You chewing gum?"

Jewel shook her head weakly.

"You stick that gum on my furniture, I make you pay for the cleaning. Hon."

The bead curtain rattled behind her like a snake's warning.

Jewel slumped in her chair and let her head fall against the backrest. "It wasn't true, what you said about the bottle on the counter," she said. "Why did you do that? Trick me, I mean, and make me order stuff I can't pay for?" Jewel closed her eyes. He talked like I was a real hero, she thought. Now she wondered if the genie really needed her help at all. What if he just wanted somebody else to get stuck washing the dishes? She wondered what her mamma would say if she looked down from heaven and saw Jewel washing dishes for the rest of her life in Solly's Restaurant. Two tears slid from the corners of her eyes and made sticky tracks into her hair. Jewel blinked at the ceiling.

On the ceiling, something winked back. There was something shiny up there, among the junk in the net. Jewel jumped to her feet.

"Oh, Mamma," she breathed. "Genie, look—I see it! A little bottle, I can see the King Solomon seal on it, it's red and—"

The rattle of the bead curtain warned her.

Jewel sat down hard as Mrs. Camgöz, carrying a tray, rolled silently into the room.

"You sure were fast," gasped Jewel.

Mrs. Camgöz laid out a place setting. Then she set down the dish of Ochtapódi Krassáto. Jewel gaped at it. Too late, she understood the meaning of that word "Ochtapódi." She judged that Krassáto meant the octopus ran into a bus.

"Enjoy," said Mrs. Camgöz, showing Jewel a smile that contained several stainless-steel teeth.

Jewel picked up her napkin and put it down again. She rearranged her knife, her fork, her spoon. She drank some water. Mrs. Camgöz did not seem in any hurry to leave her alone with her dinner.

"Uh, ma'am . . . Don't this come with salad or something? Crackers?"

"You want a cracker? That is extra."

"Well . . . How about dessert?"

"You want dessert?" Mrs. Camgöz frowned. "You don't eat your dinner and you want dessert?" Her voice rose. "I don't like little girls that waste good food, then asking for desserts." She set her knuckles on the table and leaned across at Jewel.

Jewel gabbled, "Well, I—I was waiting on my sister. You know my big sister, Ashley? She said she was going to meet me here. She told me, go ahead and order for her, too."

"You want to order something more?" The lentil eye blinked. The blue eye continued to stare. "You got money for all this?"

Jewel pretended not to hear. "What d'you think she'd like?"

"Lots of people like the cheese sandwich," said Mrs. Camgöz.

"Oh, but Ashley likes fish," lied Jewel. How about that one, uh, Excuses Marinara? What's that?"

"Skuše Marinirane. Marinated mackerel fishes. You want this?"

Marinated—that meant soaked in something, Jewel knew. She hoped Mrs. Camgöz would soak it a good long time.

"Oh yes, please," she said.

"Don't worry, we'll get it all right now," said Jewel to the genie as soon as Mrs. Camgöz was safely out of the room. " 'Cause you know why? It was the answer to my prayer. I mean, I know you got lots of powers and everything, but when something's like, the answer to a *prayer*, you know it's got to work out right." Jewel laughed. "Still, it's a good thing you're twenty feet tall and everything, 'cause I sure couldn't reach that bottle down from there myself."

"I can't do it," said the genie.

"It was so awesome," said Jewel. "I was, like, praying to my mamma, 'cause she's in heaven, you know? And then I looked up there and just *saw* it, like the answer to— What do you mean you can't do it?"

But Jewel hardly gave him time to answer. "Oh, I get it," she said, "you got to stay in that bag, huh? Well, how about if you blow it down? I can kind of hold out my skirt, like this, and you—"

"No."

"Look, it's not fair to make me do it all by myself. You made that storm outside, didn't you? I can still hear the thunder sometimes, even in here. And you said—"

"I lied," mumbled the genie.

"What?"

"I . . . exaggerated."

"You mean like, no wishes? No . . . carpet?" Jewel's throat felt tight. She sat down slowly, holding on to the edge of the table. There was gum stuck up under there. It must cost a lot to clean furniture.

"No no!" cried the genie. "Wishes—of course I can grant wishes. Carpets—pouf! Nothing to 'em. Only . . ." His voice faltered. He sighed. "Once, long ago, we genies were free spirits of the air," he told Jewel. "It is our nature to command the elements of the air, the wind, the rain, the— the lightning . . . But alas, we were insolent and unruly. We joked with the whirlwind, we buried King Solomon's washerwoman's clothesline in dust from the red desert . . . King Solomon was the wisest but not the most patient of mortals. He lost his temper. He bottled us up, and on each bottle set his seal, with the decree that never more might we use our powers to accomplish our own desires."

The genie fell silent. The silence seemed to swell inside the restaurant. There was no sound of thunder now.

"So you won't help me," said Jewel at last.

"Alas, I am bound by the seal of King Solomon to obey the owner of the bottle. Until you take the bottle for yourself, it—and I—are in the power of Mahmuzlu Camgöz. And so will you be, too," the genie added, "if you do not hasten to climb up on that table—"

"But what if she—"

"—and wish for the money to pay for your dinner," the genie concluded.

Jewel climbed up on the table. The net was still out of reach. She hauled a chair up after her. The chair didn't sit right. It teetered when she stepped up onto it. She hooked her fingers through the net.

Jewel jiggled the net. The bottle rolled closer. She stretched out her hand for it. Almost— She jiggled harder. A plastic seahorse fell through the mesh and bounced on the table, upsetting her water glass. Her fingers teased the bottle's smooth side.

"Can't you do anything?" she pleaded. "I don't mean like magic, but just as a friend?"

She did not hear the rattle of the beads.

"What is this goings-on in my dining room!"

Mrs. Camgöz advanced on Jewel's table. In her hands was the plate of cold mackerel. "You'll pay for this," she hissed, but her mouth was smiling. The blue eye glittered up at Jewel. "You think you fool me, eh? I know you don't got the money. But I let you order, yes. Yes, and now I make you pay. Twenty years you will wash dishes for me," crowed Mrs. Camgöz, "to pay for all this!" And she set the plate of fish on the table, at Jewel's feet.

"You're pretty skinny now," said Mrs. Camgöz, "but after you work a couple years, you get a good muscle."

Mrs. Camgöz reached up to grab Jewel by the ankle. Jewel tried to back away. Her chair wobbled. She grabbed on to the net with both hands.

"Quit—quit that!"

Mrs. Camgöz sidled around the table, her hands thrust forward in a wrestler's stance. Then she hesitated. Her head swiveled toward the beaded doorway. There were voices coming from the outer room. Customers.

"Why do we have to come in this dump?" whined the customer. "I don't want anything here. The floor's dirty. Look, it's totally gross."

"I told you," said a second voice, "we got to look in everywhere. She's got to be someplace around here."

"Ashley!" screamed Jewel, "Ashley, in here!"

Ashley's face appeared through the bead curtain. "Jewel?"

"You are the sister, eh?" said Mrs. Camgöz. "I certainly hope you got the money, because this one, I don't think she gots."

"What is she talking about?" said Sharon, appearing beside Ashley. "This one what?"

"Don't you be acting funny with me, hon,"

said Mrs. Camgöz, breathing so that Jewel could hear the spit rattle in her throat.

"Jewel Sue Polski," snapped Ashley, "what are you doing up on that table?"

"She is trying to escape me," bellowed Mrs. Camgöz. "Thief! Juvenile delinquent! Thirty-one dollars and ninety-two cents she owes me for this food."

The girls looked at the dishes on the table, the octopus stiffening in its sauce, the bony grin of the mackerel.

"Oh gross," said Sharon.

Ashley said, "You're telling me *my sister* ordered this slop?"

"Ashley, listen—"

"Shut up," said Ashley, "and get down from there. We're going home."

"Never!" howled Mrs. Camgöz. She seized the edge of the table and shook it. Jewel clutched at the net as the chair on the tabletop rocked, tilted, and crashed to the floor. Jewel dangled from the ceiling, her legs kicking.

"Help!" cried Jewel.

"Police!" screamed Sharon.

"Are you crazy?" hollered Ashley. "I got your stuff, Jewel. Let's get out of here."

Ashley grabbed the bundled Wonder Woman cape and turned to flee. But the cape unwound, spilling out the paper bag. The bag bounced across the floor. Mrs. Camgöz pounced on it.

"See this?" she screeched, holding up the bag. "Here is something more that girl is stealing from me!"

Then two things happened at once. Mrs. Camgöz tore open the paper bag. And the net ripped. Jewel fell in a rain of dried and plastic fish. She rolled off the table and scrabbled on hands and knees after the magic bottle. From the torn bag a little shower of gum wrappers and used paper napkins fell to the floor. There was nothing else inside.

The little bottle rolled across the floor. "So that's where you got to," muttered Mrs. Camgöz. She bent to pick it up. She did not see that, outside, storm clouds piled like black suds over the roof of the Mall. She did not see the single brilliant shaft of lightning that rent the clouds and struck the roof. But the Boom! echoed down even to Solly's Restaurant. Then all the lights went out.

Sharon shrieked. Mrs. Camgöz cursed as she groped about in the dark.

"Jewel? Jewel honey, where are you?" That was Ashley's voice.

The room seemed full of smoke, with a choking smell of Big Gob grape flavor. In the corridor of the Mall a fire alarm went off.

"*What's going on in here?*" It was a man's voice this time. A flashlight beam cut through the purple-scented gloom.

On the floor something shiny reflected the beam of light. It was the genie's magic bottle. Mrs. Camgöz and Jewel saw it at the same time. Mrs. Camgöz let out a cry of triumph that ended in a peculiar and disgustingly sticky gurgle. Then Jewel's hand closed over the bottle.

The next minute, the lights came back on.

"Everybody all right in here?" asked the man with the flashlight.

He was a neat little man, with a neatly trimmed and curled purple beard. He was round in the middle but tapered at one end to a high, shiny forehead and at the other to pointed black patent-leather boots. In fact, he was shaped very like the bottle.

"Oh my God, a police," said Sharon.

"Not exactly," said the newcomer. He wore a blue security officer's uniform with his name em-

broidered over the pocket: *Solly P. Bagge*. He
bowed slightly to the girls. "At your service," he
said.

"My sister fell," said Ashley. "I think she's
hurt."

"No, I'm not, I—"

"That horrible woman said she owed a lot of
money." Ashley pointed at Mrs. Camgöz.

Mrs. Camgöz opened her mouth to speak and
blew a bubble. She appeared to be coated with
purple gum.

"Güg," said Mahmuzlu Camgöz.

"If you'd just let me talk a minute," said Jewel,
"I could of told you all I got the money." And she
held out her hand to show one twenty-dollar bill,
one ten, one one, three quarters, one nickel, one
dime, and two pennies. Thirty-one dollars and
ninety-two cents, exactly. In her other hand she
clutched a small bottle of smoky-looking glass,
with a shiny red top.

"In that case," replied Mr. Bagge, "it is time
that I saw these young ladies home." He held
back the bead curtain for Jewel and Ashley and
Sharon to pass through.

Ashley was surprised to learn that Jewel also
had a pocketful of quarters to use in the pay

phone. Mrs. Polski, when they phoned her, said of course the girls could ride home with that nice Mr. Bagge.

"Mommom was getting kind of worried," Jewel told him. "Ashley and me live with her, you know."

"It is always wisest not to worry our loved ones," he replied.

Ashley said nothing. The truth was, she felt awed by Mr. Bagge's car, which turned out to be a Cadillac stretch limousine with a window between the back and the driver's seat. Ashley and Sharon sat together in the back, with the window rolled up. Jewel sat in front with the driver.

"This sure is a awesome car," said Jewel, settling back against the violet leather upholstery.

In the glow of the dashboard lights Mr. Bagge's smile gleamed.

"But tomorrow," said Jewel, "tomorrow, if it's not too windy, I want to try out that flying carpet."

"Your wish is my command," said Solly P. Bagge.

Toad Meets
Frankenstein

MY FRIEND TOAD lives under the cement steps that go down from our deck. Anytime I want to see him, all I do is get down by the bottom step and yell, "Hey, Toad!"

He always knows it's me. He goes, "Ugh. Ted." So I know to come on in and make myself at home. Only, if it's winter he doesn't answer, because as soon as it gets cold he creeps down into a crack underground and hibernates. That means he sleeps till spring. Miss Henderson did a unit on it in Science.

First thing, when I visit Toad, I always have to

shrink myself real small. I can do that because toads have magic. They make it in their skins so dogs won't bite them. Miss Henderson read about some boy in Texas who had to go to the hospital for sucking a toad. Miss Henderson finds a lot of neat stuff in the papers.

I say, "Hi, Toad."

That's all the name he's got, Toad. Because toad families are big—I'm talking about like hundreds and hundreds all hatching out at the same time—but they're all just called Toad. Even the girls.

I mean, in my family my dad's name is Ted, same as mine, and even with just the two of us, sometimes like I'll open his mail by mistake, because it has my name on it. Especially when there might be a chance to win a hundred million dollars.

My sister's name is Sandra, and you have to call her just that or she gets mad. Sometimes I call her Sandwich.

What I always want to do when I'm small and I'm with Toad is go down to the creek. Sometimes we hunt for treasure, because Toad is crazy about anything shiny, even stuff like the foil from gum wrappers. Or we shove a piece of bark out in

the current. Those bark boats spin around like anything, and then the water bugs have to scoot out of your way, and the crayfish look up at you from the bottom and wave their eyes. I can step right over that creek when I'm big.

One time last spring we took the lid from my lunch box through that culvert that runs under Steephill Road. A culvert is a big cement pipe. Man, is it ever dark in there and a whole lot longer than you'd think if you just walked across the road, over the top, I mean. The creek gets squeezed in the pipe so it runs real fast. Like we were slamming into sticks and all kinds of dead leaves and junk, and I was getting seriously worried that it might just fill up to the top, with no air, or we'd get stuck in all that junk. I mean, how would anybody know we were down there?

Only then I saw the light at the end of the culvert, so I yelled, "Geronimo!" And Toad went, "Dog!"

Because there was this big ugly enormous dog just waiting for us to come through. And he had teeth all over the place, like he was going to bite me in half, I mean it, while I was just laying there helpless in the water where it spreads out at the end of the pipe. But Toad started hopping up and down. You should have seen that dog's head go ᵘᵖdown, ᵘᵖdown, and his jaws going *snack! snack!* trying to catch my friend. Except by that time I'd got normal-sized again, and I got a hold of its collar. Turns out it was just Waller's puppy, who shouldn't have been way down Steephill like that. I keep telling Barry Waller he's going to lose that dog.

"Toad," I said, "looks like you just saved my life, good buddy."

And Toad said, "Ugh."

It was a real heavy-duty moment, I mean it.

But today Toad doesn't want to go to the creek, on account of it's too cold, he says. I'm sad, because I figure it'll soon be winter and I'll have to make do with Barry Waller, who's okay, I guess, except he makes things with the boogers in his nose. I am not kidding.

"Ted," says Toad to me all of a sudden, "what's the best time of year?"

"Christmas," I say without thinking, because I've still got my mind on Barry Waller's nose. Only as soon as I look at Toad I know I made a mistake. Already he's starting to swell up. Toads do this when they get excited. You can ask Miss Henderson about it if you don't believe me.

"Tell me about Christmas, Ted," he begs.

So I tell him, just a little. Colored lights. Snow on the ground, stuff like that. I know what he's really after.

"Um . . . You forgot something, Ted. You forgot Santa Claus."

So I tell him about Santa Claus, laying a finger aside of his nose. Ho ho ho. Toad's heard all this before.

"Ah! Don't forget— Don't forget—"

Presents. I tell him all about the presents, wrapped up in bright, shiny paper.

"Ugh!"

By this time Toad's swelled up so big you can't see his eyeballs anymore, and I figure any minute he'll bust out singing, Treee! Treeee! the way toads do. Only this time, instead, Toad lets out all the air, so he squashes down flat.

Then he says, sounding real sad, "Ted, I've been living here, right under this step, for twenty-nine thousand years. But I never saw Christmas." Or something like that.

Anyway, I am not really too sure how good my friend is at counting, but still I see his point. I try to imagine how I'd feel if I woke up one morning and discovered I'd slept through Christmas. That's when I have my dumb idea.

I say, "Why not come indoors with me for the winter? Soon as October comes, my mom cranks up the furnace, so it never even gets cold."

Toad looks at me and blinks. "Do you think I could, Ted?"

"Sure. You wouldn't have to go to sleep at all if you didn't want, till after Christmas."

At first it seems like a pretty good plan. Toad does okay in a box lined with wet paper towels under my bed. Only, at night he gets kind of restless and mutters a lot about the dust and why can't I find someplace else for my socks. The problem is, my mom has this absolute Thing about vacuuming under my bed. Toad takes it pretty hard, even harder than my mom, actually. Afterward I notice he doesn't look too good, kind of pale.

So then I begin to worry my friend Toad should go back under the step. I ask Miss Henderson, and she says animals are better off in nature. I explain this to Toad, but he just gives me this gumball-eye look. Toads can be pretty stubborn, I guess.

I put him in the bathroom, because we have two bathrooms upstairs, so my mom would never have to bother with him, and anyway, it's

damper in there. Miss Henderson says amphibi-
ans have to stay moist. There's the soap place in
the shower stall that is just the right size. Only,
my sister, Sandra, takes him for a bar of Zest or
something. She is not a very relaxed kind of person.

My mom makes me stay in my room until I
can apologize to my sister, which is totally un-
fair. Because, after all, it was Toad that got
dropped.

I am concerned about my friend. I say, "Well,
it was a good try, buddy, but maybe if you
got some sleep you could be up in time for
Easter."

I don't like to pass on any of the stuff my mom
said about finding That Creature in the house
again. Because I think you should always be sensitive about a person's feelings even if they are an
amphibian.

But Toad just looks at me and blinks, with his
eyeballs going right down inside his head, the
way toads do. Miss Henderson says that's how
they swallow.

So then I think maybe Toad better go down to
the basement. My mom hates the basement. And
for a while he does pretty good. We even get bugs
down there sometimes, which is a good thing,

because I notice how he's getting kind of skinny-looking and wrinkled.

The only trouble is, we get field mice in the basement sometimes, too. So Sandra's cat, Puffie, is always hanging around behind the furnace, hoping. Puffie can't bite my friend on account of his skin, but she does kind of lean her paw on him one time and look at him with those mean cat eyes.

I don't know what's going on right at first, because I'm real busy upstairs getting ready for trick or treating. It's Halloween. Only, this year Mom says will I mind very much going around with my sister Sandra and her friends, because my parents are all set to go to this big costume dress-up party they're having for grownups at the firehouse.

My dad is Frankenstein, and actually by the time my sister Sandra gets through with him, and the green makeup, he looks pretty cool. I let him use some stuff of mine, too, because I have nose putty that works great, and there are these great big plastic bolts for sticking out of the sides of his head. They used to twist into a tool bench set I had when I was two. My mom saves a lot of stuff like that.

Sandra's friends arrive, but they aren't ready

yet, they never are, so I go down to the basement to check on Toad before I go out for the evening. That's when I have to rescue him from that dumb Puffie.

I take Toad upstairs into the den and put him on top of the TV set. I switch on the TV, with the sound turned down all the way. The top of the set gets nice and warm. Toad likes that. There's some undersea program on. I watch a frogman swim round and round in the green water. Toad crawls to the edge of the set to watch the screen flicker.

"Colored lights," he says.

"Uh—yeah. Listen, buddy, about tonight—"

I wish I could take him with me, but it's real cold. Too cold for October.

"Ah," says Toad. "Tonight."

I think he's looking at me kind of funny. I wonder if he's guessed what I'm going to tell him, about how it's not safe for him in our house. How he'll have to go back under the step.

Just then my dad comes in. He's all rigged out for the party, with the bolts in his head. Only he's got his pipe still stuck in his teeth, which spoils the effect some. He's carrying two big plastic bags of trick-or-treat candy. Luckily he doesn't spot my toad but just dumps the candy into the bowl on top of the TV. He stands there for a minute, smoking and trying to scratch his nose without peeling off the putty. Then he sits down in front of the TV and closes his eyes.

And Toad just busts out singing, "Treee! *Treeee!*"

"Cut that out!" I hiss. "You want to wake him up?"

"Oh, Ted," he sings, "how tall he is! How splendid! *Treeee!*"

"Huh? Who?"

"Santa Claus!" Toad's eyes are like yellow stars. He's looking at my dad. "He is Santa Claus, isn't he?"

So what am I supposed to say? I say, "I guess so." I mean, it's not exactly lying.

"You never told me he was green, Ted."

"It was a surprise."

"And bumps. He has bumps, Ted."

"Yeah."

"I had no idea." Toad sighs blissfully. My dad lets out a little snore. Ho ho ho.

Toad says, "And is this all—all for me?"

He means the Halloween candy.

I say, "Sure, Toad. Merry Christmas, buddy."

My friend closes his eyes. He says, "Guess I'll be getting home now."

"Guess so."

Toad opens his eyes. "Ted?"

"Yeah?"

"Do you think it will snow tonight?"

"You never know, Toad."

He closes his eyes again. "Merry Christmas, Ted."

"See you in the spring, Toad."